Anonymous

Twenty Years of the Ethical Movement

in New York and other cities - 1876-1896

Anonymous

Twenty Years of the Ethical Movement
in New York and other cities - 1876-1896

ISBN/EAN: 9783337406158

Printed in Europe, USA, Canada, Australia, Japan

Cover: Foto ©Andreas Hilbeck / pixelio.de

More available books at **www.hansebooks.com**

1876   1896

Twenty Years

OF THE

Ethical Movement

IN

New York and Other Cities.

———————

PHILADELPHIA :

S. BURNS WESTON, 1305 Arch Street.

1896.

CONTENTS.

PRINTED BY INNES & SON, PHILADELPHIA

ADDRESS OF MAY 15TH, 1876.

At Standard Hall, New York.*

FOR a long time the conviction has been dimly felt in the community that, without prejudice to existing institutions, the legal day of weekly rest might be employed to advantage for purposes affecting the general good. During the past few years this conviction has steadily gained in force and urgency, until lately a number of gentlemen have been impelled to give it shape and practical effect.

Conceiving that in so laudable an enterprise they may justly hope for the sympathy and co-operation of the friends of progress, they have invited you to join in their deliberations this evening, and upon me devolves the task of stating, as frankly and plainly as may be, the end we have in view and the means by which its achievement will be attempted. At such a time, when we are about to set forth on a path hitherto untried and likely to lead our lives in a new direction, it appears eminently desirable and proper that we should, in the first place, briefly review the public and private life of the day, in order to determine whether the essential elements that make up the happiness of states and indi-

---

* Given at the meeting called to organize the first Society for Ethical Culture.

viduals are all duly provided, and if not, where the need lies and how it can best be supplied.

On the face of it, our age exhibits certain distinct traits in which it excels all of its predecessors. Eulogies on the nineteenth century are familiar to our ears, and orators delight to descant upon all the glorious things which it has achieved. Its railways, its printing presses, its increased comforts and refined luxuries—all these are undeniable facts, and yet it is true none the less, that great and unexpected evils have followed in the train of our successes, and that the moral improvement of nations and their individual components has not kept pace with the march of intellect and the advance of industry. Before the assaults of criticism many ancient strongholds of faith have given way, and doubt is fast spreading even into circles where its expression is forbidden. Morality, long accustomed to the watchful tutelage of faith, finds this connection loosened or severed, while no new protector has arisen to champion her rights, no new instruments been created to enforce her lessons among the people. As a consequence we behold a general laxness in regard to obligations the most sacred and dear. An anxious unrest, a fierce craving desire for gain has taken possession of the commercial world, and in instances no longer rare the most precious and permanent goods of human life have been madly sacrificed in the interests of momentary enrichment.

Far be it from me, indeed, to disparage the importance of commerce or to slight its just claims as an agent in the service of humanity. In a country of such recent civilization as ours, whose almost limitless treasures of material wealth invite the risks of capital and the industry of labor, it is but natural that material interests should absorb the attention of the people to a degree elsewhere unknown. But all the more on this account it is necessary to provide a powerful check and counterpoise, lest the pursuit of gain be enhanced to an importance never rightfully its own, lest, in proportion as we enhance our comfort and well-being, comfort and well-being become the main objects of existence, and life's grander motives and meanings be forgotten. We have already transgressed the limit of safety, and the present disorders of our time are but precursors of other and imminent dangers. The rudder of our ship has ceased to move obedient to the helm. We are drifting on the seething tide of business, each one absorbed in holding his own in the giddy race of competition, each one engrossed in immediate cares and seldom disturbed by thoughts of larger concerns and ampler interests. Even our domestic life has lost much of its former warmth and geniality. The happy spirits of unaffected content and simple endearment are sadly leaving our low-burnt hearth-fires. Fagged and careworn the merchant returns to his home in the evening. He finds his children weary. His own mind is distracted. In these troublous times business cares not unfrequently dog him even into the seclusion of the family circle. How, then, is he to discover that tranquil leisure, that serenity of soul which he needs to be a true father to his little ones. He cannot form their characters ; he cannot justly estimate their needs. Perforce he leaves their education in part to the wife—and modern wives have their own troubles and are often but little fitted to undertake so arduous a task—in part he must abandon it to strangers.

It has been said that the modern world is divided
between the hot and hasty pursuit of affairs in the hours
of labor, and the no less eager chase of pleasure in the
hours of leisure.   But even our pleasures are calculated
and business like.   We measure our enjoyments by the
sum expended.   Our salons are often little better than
bazars of fashion.   We wander about festive halls, chew-
ing artificial phrases which we neither believe nor desire
to be believed.   We breathe a stale and insipid perfume
from which the spirit of joy has fled.   The brief ex-
hilaration of the dance, the physical stimulus of wine
and of food, the nervous excitement of a game of hazard,
perhaps these make up the sum total of enjoyment in
by far the majority of our so-called parties of pleasure.
Surely, of all things melancholy in American life, American mirth is the most melancholy!   And were it not
for Music—that divine comforter which sometimes wins
us to higher flights of emotion and speaks in its own
wordless language of an ideal beauty and harmony far
transcending the prosy aspirations to which we confess—
our life would be utterly blank and colorless.   We
should be like the bees that build, they know not why,
and hive honey whose sweetness they never enjoy.
There is a great and crying evil in modern society.   It
is want of purpose   It is that narrowness of vision
which shuts out the wider vistas of the soul.   It is the
absence of those sublime emotions which, wherever they
arise, do not fail to exalt and consecrate existence.
True. the void and hollowness of which we speak is
covered over by a fair exterior.   Men distil a subtle
sort of intoxication from the ceaseless flow and shifting
changes of affairs, and the deeper they quaff the more

potent for awhile is the efficacy of the charm. But there comes a time of rude awakening. A great crisis sweeps over the land. The sinews of trade are relaxed, the springs of wealth are sealed. Old houses, whose foundations seemed as lasting as the hills, give way before the storm. Reverse follows reverse. The man whose energies were hitherto expended in the accumulation of wealth finds himself ruined by the wayside. His business has proved a failure. Is his life, too, therefore a failure? Is there no other object for which he can still live and labor? Nor need we turn to such seasons of unusual disaster in order to exhibit the instability and insufficiency of the common motives of life. There are accidents to which we all are alike exposed and which none, however favored by fortune, can hope to avoid. A blight comes upon our affections. The dearest objects of our solicitude are taken from us. Our home is darkened with the deep darkness of the shadow of death. In such hours, what is to keep our heart from freezing in chill despair, to keep our head high and our step firm, if it be not the deep-seated, long and carefully matured conviction, that man was set into the world to perform a great and unselfish work, independent of his comfort, independent even of his happiness, and that in its performance alone he can find his true solace, his lasting reward? To arouse such courage, to build up and buttress such a conviction, would not this be a loyal and much-needed service?

Where the roots of private virtue are diseased, the fruit of public probity cannot but be corrupt.

When on the 30th of April, 1789, General Washington was for the first time inducted into the presidential

office in this city of New York, he declared that "the
national policy would be laid in the pure and immutable
principles of private morality." And he appealed to
the wisdom and integrity of those first legislators whom
the country had chosen under its new constitution, as a
pledge and safeguard of the Republic's future welfare.
Could he return to us now in this season of jubilation,
how sadly altered would he find the condition of our
affairs! There is not a morning's journal that reaches
us that is not besmirched with tales of theft and per-
jury. The very names that ought to be held up as lumi-
naries of honor have become bywords of villany, and
the foul stench of corruption fills our public offices.
See how the Nation, in this the festal epoch of her marriage to Liberty, stands blackened with the crimes of
her first dignitaries, and hides her head in shame before
the nations! And for what have these miserable men
bartered away their honor and that of the people? For
the same unhallowed und unreasoning desire of rapid
gain which has brought such heavy disaster upon the
commercial world : to support the extravagance of their
households; to deepen, perhaps, the potations of a
carousal! Statesmen and philanthropists are busy sug-
gesting remedies for the cure of these great evils. But
the renovation of our Civil Service, the reform of our
Primaries, and whatever other measures may be devised,
they all depend in the last instance upon the fidelity of
those to whom their execution must be intrusted. They
will all fail unless the root of the evil be attacked, unless
the conscience of men be aroused, the confusion of right
and wrong checked, and the loftier purposes of our

being again brought powerfully home to the hearts of
the people.

I have spoken of our private needs and of the larger
claims of the public well-being.   But another question
now presents itself, fraught with deeper and tenderer
meanings even than these.   The children, the heirs of
all the great future, what shall we do for them ?   Into
this world of sinfulness and sorrow, with its thousand-
fold snares and sore temptations, shall we let their white
souls go forth without even an effort to keep them stain-
less ?   Do you not struggle and toil and trouble, that
you may leave them, when you die, some little store of
earthly goods, something to make their life easier, perhaps, than yours has been—that you may turn to your
long sleep, knowing that your children shall not want
bread ?   And for that which is far more precious than
bread shall we make no provision ?   When your bodies
have long been mouldering in the grave, they will live,
men and women, fighting the world's battles and bearing
the world's burdens like yourselves.   Would you not
feel the benign assurance that they will be true men and
noble women ? that the fair name which you transmit to
them will ever be clean in their keeping ? that they will
be strong even in adversity, because they believe in the
destiny of mankind and in the dignity of man ?   And
what efforts do we make to attain this end ?   We teach
them to repeat some scattered verses of the Bible, some
doctrine which at their time of life they can but half
comprehend at best ; and then, at thirteen or fourteen,
at the very age when doubt begins to arise in the young
heart, when in its inefficient gropings towards the light,
youth stands most in need of friendly help and counsel

we send them out to shift for themselves. Is it with such an armor that we can equip them for the hard hand-to-hand fight of after-life? Or do you conceive a magic charm, a talismanic power to guard from evil, to reside in these empty words which you teach your children's lips to spell?

Already complaints are multiplying on every hand that that most gracious quality of all that adorns the age of childhood—the quality of reverence—is fast fading from our schools and households; that the old-time respect for father and mother is diminished, and grown rarer and more uncertain. Twenty years ago, what high prophecies did we not hear of the future of the generation then growing up! What inspiriting promises of the full bloom into which the still closed petals of their life would one day open! Have the young men of the present day fulfilled these pledges? Has the passive reverence of the child developed into the active aspiration of the man? Do you find them in the higher walks of their professions—I say take them as a whole, and set aside a few brilliant exceptions—have they illustrated the sterling qualities of the race they sprang from, the dearer virtues of our common humanity? We have sown the seeds of long neglect. We are but reaping the bitter Sodom fruit of dead hopes and fair promises turned to ashes. And now I need not appeal to your business instincts to show that any change, if it is to come—and a change must come—can be brought about only, first, by united effort; secondly, by applying that great principle which has been the secret of the enormous progress of industry and com-

merce in the past century—the salutary principle of
division of labor.

You do not build your own houses, nor make your
own garments, nor bake your own bread, simply because
you know that if you were to attempt all these things
they would all be more or less ill done.   But you go to
the builder to build your house, to the baker to bake
your bread, because you know that in limitation there is
power, that limitation and combination are the essentials
of success.   On this account you limit your own energies to some one of the many callings which society has
marked out, and by combination with your fellows, are
certain that in proportion as your own part is well per-
formed, you may command the best services in every
department in exchange for what you offer.   What is
true of material wants is also pertinent in the case of
intellectual needs.   If you desire information on some
point of law, you are not likely to ponder over the pon-
derous tomes of legal writers in order to obtain the
knowledge you seek, by your own unaided efforts.   But
you apply to some one in the profession in whose abili-
ties you see reason to confide.   The same holds good in
every department of knowledge.   In every case you
turn to the specialist, trusting that, if from any source at
all, you will obtain from him the best of what you need.
Nor is it otherwise in education.   For though you possess a sufficient knowledge of the branches taught in
our schools, yet you are well aware that it is one thing
to know, and quite another to impart knowledge.   And
so again you step aside in your own persons to intrust
the office of training your children in the arts and sciences to an instructor, to a specialist.   And if all this

be true, then it follows that, if the *moral* elevation of ourselves, the *moral* training of our children, be also an object worth achieving, ay, if it be the highest object of our life on earth, then we dare not trust for its accomplishment to the sparse and meager hours which the busy world leaves us. Then, here as elsewhere, society must set apart some who shall be specialists in this, who shall throw all the energy of temper, all the ardor of aspiration, all the force of heart and intellect, into this difficult but ever glorious work.

The past speaks to us in a thousand voices, warning and comforting, animating and stirring to action. What its great thinkers have thought and written on the deepest problems of life, shall we not hear and enjoy? The future calls upon us to prepare its way. Dare we fail to answer its solemn summons ?

And now for all these purposes we propose to unite our efforts in association, and to set apart one day of the seven as a day of weekly reunion,—a day of ease, that shall come to repair the wasted energies of body and mind, and whereon, in the enjoyment of perfect tranquillity, the finer relations of our being may find time to acquaint us with their sweet and friendly influences. What that day shall be it is not for us to determine. The usages of American society have long since settled that practically it is, and for the present at least can be, only the Sunday. This is the sole day of respite whereon the great machine of business pauses in its operations, and leaves you to direct your thoughts to other than immediate cares. In the ancient synagogue the Monday and Thursday, in the early church the Wednesday and Friday, were set apart for purposes of higher instruction, over and above the stated Sabbath meetings. If the Monday, the Thursday, the Wednesday, or the Friday had in our community been eliminated from the week of labor, we should accept any one of them with the same willingness. The name of the day is immaterial. It is the opportunity it offers with which alone we are here concerned. And how others see fit to spend the day is foreign to our consideration, and whatever mischievous construction may be placed upon our work will quickly be dispelled, depend upon it, by the character and testimony of the work itself. The young men, at all events, can desist from labor upon no other day than the Sunday. Heads of firms may, if they see fit, incur the risk of taking an exceptional position in the business community ; but the young men, who depend upon others for patronage and employment, cannot in this matter select their own course, and if they attempt it will be met by innumerable and insuperable obstacles at every step. But it has been urged by some that the Sunday should be devoted to the intimate intercourse of the domestic circle, from which our merchants are so often debarred at other times. This is an honorable motive, surely, which we are bound to respect. But is it, indeed, believed that a single hour spent in serious contemplation will at all unduly infringe upon the time proper to the home circle ? Rather will it give a higher tone to all our occupations, and lend a newer and fresher zest even to those enjoyments which we need and seek.

The exercises of our meetings are to be simple and devoid of all ceremonial and formalism. They are to consist of a *lecture* mainly, and, as a pleasing and grateful auxiliary, of *music* to elevate the heart and give rest to the feelings. The object of the lectures shall be twofold : First, to illustrate the history of human aspirations, its monitions and its examples ; to trace the origin of many of those errors of the past whose poisonous tendrils still cling to the life of the present, but also to exhibit its pure and bright examples, and so *to enrich the little sphere of our earthly existence by showing the grander connections in which it everywhere stands with the large life of the race.* For, as the taste is refined in viewing some work of ideal beauty—some statue vivid with divine suggestion, some painting glowing with the painter's genius—so in the contemplation of large thoughts do we ourselves enlarge, and the soul for a time takes on the grandeur and excellency of whatever it truly admires. Secondly, it will be the object of the lecturers to set forth a standard of duty, to discuss our practical duties in the practical present, to make clear the responsibilities which our nature as moral beings imposes upon us in view of the political and social evils of our age, and also to dwell upon those high and tender consolations which the modern view of life does not fail to offer us even in the midst of anguish and affliction. Do not fear, friends, that a priestly office after a new fashion will be thus introduced. The office of the public teacher is an unenviable and thankless one. Few are there that will leave the secure seclusion of the scholar's life, the peaceful walks of literature and learning, to stand out a target for the criticism of unkind and hostile minds. Moreover, the lecturer is but an instrument in your hands. It is not to him you listen, but to those countless others that speak to you through him in strange tongues, of which he is no more than the humble interpreter. And what he fails to express, what no language that was ever spoken on earth can express—those nameless yearnings of the soul for something better and happier far than aught we know of—Music will give them utterance and solve and soothe them.

We propose to entirely exclude prayer and every form of ritual. Thus shall we avoid even the appearance of interfering with those to whom prayer and ritual, as a mode of expressing religious sentiment, are dear. And on the other hand we shall be just to those who have ceased to regard them as satisfactory and dispensed with them in their own persons. Freely do I own to this purpose of reconciliation, and candidly do I confess that it is my dearest object to exalt the present movement above the strife of contending sects and parties, and at once to occupy that *common ground* where we may all meet, believers and unbelievers, for purposes in themselves lofty and unquestioned by any. Surely it is time that a beginning were made in this direction. For more than three thousand years men have quarrelled concerning the formulas of their faith. The earth has been drenched with blood shed in this cause, the face of day darkened with the blackness of the crimes perpetrated in its name. There have been no direr wars than religious wars, no bitterer hates than religious hates, no fiendish cruelty like religious cruelty; no baser baseness than religious baseness. It has destroyed the peace of families, turned the father against the son, the brother against the brother. And for what? Are we any nearer to unanimity? On the contrary, diversity within the churches and without has never been so widespread as at present. Sects and factions are multiplying on every hand, and every new schism is but the parent of a dozen others. And it must be so. Let us make up our minds to that.

The freedom of thought is a sacred right of every individual man, and diversity will continue to increase with the progress, refinement, and differentiation of the human intellect. But if difference be inevitable, nay, welcome in thought, there is a sphere in which unanimity and fellowship are above all things needful. Believe or disbelieve as ye list—we shall at all times respect every honest conviction. But be one with us where there is nothing to divide—in action. *Diversity in the creed, unanimity in the deed!* This is that practical religion from which none dissents. This is that platform broad enough and solid enough to receive the worshipper and the "infidel." This is that common ground where we may all grasp hands as brothers, united in mankind's common cause. The Hebrew prophets said of old, To serve Jehovah is to make your hearts pure and your hands clean from corruption, to help the suffering, to raise the oppressed. Jesus of Nazareth said that he came to comfort the weary and heavy laden. The philosopher affirms that the true service of religion is the unselfish service of the common weal. There is no difference among them all. There is no difference in the law. *But so long have they quarrelled concerning the origin of law that the law itself has fallen more and more into abeyance.* For indeed, as it is easier to say, "I do not believe," and have done with it, so also it is easier to say, "I believe," and thus to

bribe one's way into heaven, as it were, than to fulfil
nobly our human duties with all the daily struggle and
sacrifice which they involve. "The proposition is peace!"
Peace to the warring sects and their clamors, peace also
of heart and mind unto us—that peace which is the
fruition of purest and highest liberty. Let religion un-
furl her white flag over the battlegrounds of the past,
and turn the fields she has desolated so long into sunny
gardens and embowered retreats. Thither let her call
the traveler from the dusty high-road of life to breathe
a softer, purer air, laden with the fragrance of the
flowers of wonderland, and musical with sweet and
restful melody. There shall he bathe his spirit in the
crystal waters of the well of truth, and thence proceed
again upon his journey with fresher vigor and new
elasticity.

Ah, why should there be any more the old dividing
line between man and his brother-man? why should the
fires of prejudice flare up anew between us? why should
we not maintain this common ground which we have
found at last, and hedge it round, and protect it—the
stronghold of freedom and of all the humanities for the
long years to come? Not since the days of the Reformation has there been a crisis so great as this through
which the present age is passing. The world is dark
around us and the prospect seems deepening in gloom.
And yet there is light ahead. On the volume of the
past in starry characters it is written—the starry legend
greets us shining through the misty vistas of the future
—that the great and noble shall not perish from among
the sons of men, that the truth will triumph in the end,
and that even the humblest of her servants may in this

become the instruments of unending good. We are aiding in laying the foundations of a mighty edifice, whose completion shall not be seen in our day, no, nor in centuries upon centuries after us. But happy are we, indeed, if we can contribute even the least towards so high a consummation. The time calls for action. Up, then, and let us do our part faithfully and well. And oh, friends, our children's children will hold our memories dearer for the work which we begin this hour.

TWENTIETH ANNIVERSARY

OF THE

SOCIETY FOR ETHICAL CULTURE

OF NEW YORK,

CARNEGIE HALL, FRIDAY EVENING, MAY 15TH, 1896.*

ADDRESS BY ALFRED R. WOLFF.†

Well may the joyous strains of solemn music fill the
air, well may the glorious beauty of blooming flowers
greet the eye, for we are here to-night to celebrate a
great occasisn.   Oh, that our feeble speech could as fittingly translate the gladness of the heart !

Imbued with a love for the Society and for the principles it inculcates, we rejoice in our existence these twenty
years.   We rejoice in what has been accomplished in
the past ; we rejoice still more in the greater and better
things to be accomplished in the future.   We rejoice that
our movement has spread and is spreading on fruitful
soil here and abroad, in the new world and in the old.   We
rejoice that new and strong leaders have espoused our

---

* The Hall was beautifully decorated with flowers, and classical music
was rendered, before and after each address, by the Musical Art Society
of New York, under the direction of Mr. Frank Damrosch.

† On behalf of the members of the Society for Ethical Culture of New
York.

cause. We rejoice that our own distinguished leader,
he who called this great movement into existence and
who has been its fountain source, our trusted and beloved
guide these many years, is with us to-day, in the prime
of his power, undimmed in intellect, ripe in experience,
rich in soul, his life bound up with and consecrated to
the cause.

Those of us who, looking backward, remember the
many prophecies of our speedy and effective dissolution,
cannot but feel that the very fact of having existed
twenty years counts for much, for in all this time there
has been no backsliding, no change of principle, no
change of heart, merely a healthy development and a
vigorous growth.

We hold in grateful memory the small band of earnest
men who launched the ship and helped steer it in the
right course. We glory in their enthusiasm and self-
sacrifice, and, kindled by their example, we resolve that
henceforth our efforts will be more worthy of theirs.

We are attached to our Society. We believe in the
principles it represents. We recognize that nothing
should be left undone to discover the right. We favor
the broadest inquiry, we court the deepest philosophy,
the closest introspection, but the mere formulation of
the right in the abstract does not satisfy our needs. We
know that the right must be translated practically into
every action of our lives. Our home life must show
plain evidence of this, so must our career in business or
in the professions. Our duties as citizens must be conceived in a high spirit, and the great social reforms and
humanitarian problems of the world must claim our
hearty co-operation and loving devotion. We may be

frail and weak and not always succeed, but we recognize the obligation, even when we score a failure.

In the existing complex and interwoven organization of society the individual is dependent on his fellowmen, and right living is difficult, not to say impossible, if there be not a congenial and responsive environment. It is this which makes association of those who would discover and act the right so important; it is the answer to those who would favor individualism in ethics and discourage societies for ethical culture. The moral hero may need no impulse from without, for him temptations may not exist, but the ordinary mortal, anxious to live his part well, requires spiritual companions, the hand of fellowship, the strength of good example, encouragement, and a sympathetic surrounding. Then, too, the social conditions are still so bad, there is so much remedial and curative work to be done, that only co-operation and the active association of many can accomplish even slight changes in the right direction. Our individualistic moral hero may lead a beautiful inspiring life passively, but to do so with equal success actively he cannot ignore the outer world, but must co-operate with other spirits whose aims are high. We, members of the Society for Ethical Culture, know we are but ordinary mortals who need the light of wisdom and inspiration which others wiser and better can give us; who need the strength which comes from high endeavor, from union in a good cause, the fellowship of congenial souls, and, therefore, we are banded together. We feel we are better fitted to do our part in the world's work because of this union.

On this, our twentieth anniversary, it is pardonable to note with gratification that we have been enabled to con tribute our little share to some important educational and social reforms.   Our Workingman's School, in which the training of the hand, the mind, and the heart is brought into one harmonious union, in which culture in its broadest sense is the goal, is rated by educators the world over as a pioneer institution of undoubted success, a far-reaching influence for the good.   The district nursing system, which has brought relief to many sufferers has proved of such value that it has become a regular institution of the leading Dispensaries.   We might recall much other important work, but let us rather in this hour of joy and happiness feel that what has been done is as nothing to what has been left undone and still remains to be done.   Let us rather contemplate the past in the spirit of consecration and dedication to the future, resolved that henceforth we will strive to do better, and, above all, to be better.   For it is the inward peace which we must gain : so to live that we feel in touch with the divine purpose which permeates tne world. To the extent we realize this, to that extent do we realize the spirit of religion, which should be the flower of an ethical inspiration, of an ethical life.   The more our souls are filled with and guided by the love of the right, the more our every action and principle in life is the outgrowth and the logical result of this spirit, the greater will be our achievement, the greater our peace, and there will come to us a faith in the triumph of the right which is certainly akin to, if it be not, religion.

Because this is our belief, therefore are we members of the Society.   To us the Society represents a vital issue and a vital force.   It is not a club, it is not a purely secular organization ; we cherish it as an aid and a necessity to our soul-life.   It represents to us a church, teaching no tenet inconsistent with the severest logic and the profoundest science, but still a church, for it recalls to us our relation to the life universal and bids us do our part fittingly, manfully, well, despite any discouragements, despite any hardships, despite any temptations.   It teaches the ultimate triumph of the right, and that it is our part to be a factor and an agent to help bring about this triumph.

I have spoken as a member of the crew.   The ship we sail is steering for the City of the Light.   Far distant as we are from the coveted shore, our trained and faithful captains feel its magnetic influence.   Inspired, they describe to us their vision and bid us follow them and work with renewed, untiring energy.   We know we cannot reach the shore, but we are happy in the thought that our work may bring the ship nearer its destination.   It is a noble cruise.   We recall to-night that we have sailed the ship for twenty years ; we have made some headway on the voyage.   Privileged to be of the crew, we proclaim our eagerness to continue the voyage bound for the same goal, under the same fine guidance, our hearts full of joy that we can do our small part in the onward course of the good ship.   With Longfellow we say :

> " In spite of rock and tempest's roar,
> In spite of false lights on the shore,
> Sail on, nor fear to breast the sea !
> Our hearts, our hopes, are all with thee,
> Our hearts, our hopes, our prayers, our tears,
> Our faith triumphant o'er our fears,
> Are all with thee—all with thee !"

ADDRESS BY WILLIAM M. SALTER.

Members of the Society for Ethical Culture, this is a glad day for you here. But it is my privilege to say that beyond the city of New York there are those who are rejoicing with you. This is a local anniversary, but it awakens a national, I might say, an international interest. You of this Society have started a stream of influence— and the stream may be stronger at its fountain head than anywhere else—but it is a stream that has reached other cities and other lands and has refreshed dry and thirsty hearts wherever it has gone.

Six years after you began here, a kindred society sprang up in Chicago. Two years later, a society arose in Philadelphia. In one year more the St. Louis Ethical Society was born. And the proudest testimony which these spiritual children of your leader could give to him is that so much of his vitality and vigor has passed into them that even without him they could hold a successful convention—in some respects the most successful convention the American Ethical Societies ever had— recently in St. Louis (in connection with the tenth anniversary of the local Society). A few years later yet, the West London Ethical Society formed itself under the leadership of Dr. Coit, and since then three other societies have been formed in that great city. Germany, too, has given birth to an ethical movement, and through Germany the movement has gone to Austria, Italy and Switzerland. France has an at least similar movement, though not so directly an offspring of the American movement as those in other countries. All of these societies are rejoicing in your anniversary to-day, or would, if they knew of it.

Out of several messages that have been received I will read these two :

VIENNA, May 15, 1896.

Felix Adler, New York:
Heartiest wishes from Austrian Ethical Society.

BREZINA, *President.*

BERLIN, May 15, 1896.

Felix Adler, New York:
To to-day's celebration the German Society for Ethical Culture sends most cordial good wishes and fraternal gratitude.

As I came over on the train from Philadelphia this morning I read the address made by your leader in Standard Hall just twenty years ago. I marveled at the clear vision and the firm hand with which he portrayed the evils of the time which your Society was designed to meet, and when he said at the close : " And oh, friends, our childrens' children will hold our memories dearer for the work which we begin this hour," I wondered if he had any idea of children in the larger and less local sense, such as those to whom I have referred. Children from afar as well as those in New York, children whom you may never see, as well as those growing up under your eyes, rise up in spirit and bless you for the bold, brave stand taken by your leader twenty years ago, and for the ready and ever loyal response which you have given to his appeals. Few men, I think, have accomplished so much in twenty years as Felix Adler, particularly in so difficult a field as that of moral reform ; and, after all, the work is but in its beginnings.

One actual problem now is to hold the ethical movement together.   It has grown so large, it is spreading so rapidly, that it is even difficult to keep track of it—not to say, hold it together in bonds of conscious fellowship.   With the new day we need new institutions. We need what I might call a Home and Foreign Secretary who should keep in touch with the societies, old and new, and keep them in touch with one another.   We do not wish to have the movement disintegrate and split up into mere local, self-centered, organizations, but to remain one body and to have a common spirit and a common life.   There is danger of irresponsible societies arising and doing injury as well as good to our cause, unless we are alert to these needs and aggressive in meeting them.

And then how great the need of leaders !   There is not a large city in our land in which an Ethical Society might not be planted, had we the right men to put at their head.   And in a new movement, leaders are absolutely necessary.   Interest, even enthusiasm, are not sufficient.   There must be intelligent direction.   What an opportunity is thus open to young men—yes, I might add, young women !   The fact is our movement is growing beyond our power to wisely direct it—at once a splendid tribute to you who begot it and yet a matter for anxious concern and serious consideration.

Yes, friends of the New York Society, there is just one thing that gives me disappointment in these twenty years of your history.   You and your leader have left a noble record of yourselves in the large undertakings of public utility you have set on foot in this city, in the elevated utterances from your platform, in the example and the help you have lent to sister societies elsewhere.

But you have not given us another ethical leader out of your own midst. And we need one. We need one born and bred under the influences that have only come to the rest of us in later years, and that, had they come earlier, might have made us twice the men that we are. Yes, why shall I not say it? We need another son of Israel, one of that race to whom imagination and genius and eloquent speech come like gifts of nature, who can fire the heart as perhaps we of colder blood cannot, and of whom, according to an authority revered all over the Christian world, human salvation comes. Would there were within reach of my voice to-night some one who in all humility, and yet in all confidence, might heed the call, on whom the rich mantle of your leader might fall and who might do elsewhere the great and beneficent work which he has been doing here! If I could drop a thought of this sort into fruitful ground here I should count myself happy indeed.

Society for Ethical Culture of New York, your friends and children from near and from far greet you through me now; we want more like you, we want more leaders like yours!

ADDRESS BY M. M. MANGASARIAN.

Not having received the manuscript of Mr. Mangasarian's address, we can only give a brief resume of what he said. He began by saying that he wished to congratulate the New York Society upon the great work they had achieved, and hoped that their devotion to the cause and their example would inspire the sister societies to larger action. He wanted to see the idea of the movement more widely spread in this country and to have it stand for large affirmations, for affirmations that would in time create an ethical liturgy in which both lecturer and congregation could take part. The aim of our movement is not to rob the world of faith and hope, but to rationalize and elevate them. The message of ethics is not a message of doubt, of uncertainty, but of positive faith in the moral verities of life. Ethics is synonymous with hope, not despair; it is a religion to all who believe that the moral life is the supreme end of human endeavor.

ADDRESS BY FELIX ADLER.

It is under the stress of deep feeling that I address you to-night, at the close of the second decade of our existence. A score of years has passed since a small company of men and women—a mere handful—agreed to associate themselves together for purposes which seemed to them exceedingly, nay, incomparably, significant. The seed that was then planted has not perished. The words then spoken have had a certain resonance. We have heard this evening echoes of them from across the sea. And yet this is no occasion for self-congratulation. Truly, the legend of St. Christopher is applicable in a wider sense than its literal meaning would imply—the legend of the man who undertook to carry the Christ-

child on his shoulders across a stream. And the deeper
he entered into the water the heavier became the burden
which he had assumed so lightly at the start, until it
pressed upon him like a mountain, and he threatened to
succumb beneath its weight. Such is the experience of
all who, in the sanguine days of youth, have assumed
the divine burden of a reformation of any kind ; and
there is no salvation for them unless their strength shall
increase in proportion as the load increases. This,
then, is an occasion useful and needful for us, that we
may renew our strength, our courage, our hope. And
we can best do so by going back for a moment to the
source from which we derived our original impetus, by
reviewing the reasons which led to the formation of our
Society, by coming face to face with those principles
which were the incentives that prompted us. It is said
that the mere sight of the gods is rejuvenating. So,
also, is the contemplation of god-like ideals.

The motive that prompted the formation of the Society was the desire for an institution which, for its
members, should take the place of a church. The
church, in its broadest sense, has a social function.
The function of the church is to present the ideal of
society as it ought to be, in the midst of human society,
imperfect as it actually is. It is also to be a fair pat-
tern, a living embodiment, a suggestive type, of more
ideal relationships than those which commonly prevail.
As the ideals of society differ, so do churches differ.
But the church, in the widest meaning of the word—
call it by whatever name you please—is not perishable.
It will last as long as the state lasts, or, rather, until
it shall have absorbed the state into itself. Now the

church, it should be remembered, has a service to render to the families as well as to the individuals of which
it is composed. The family life, if it is to be thoroughly
wholesome and fine, requires the consecration of conscious connection with the larger social life that sur-
rounds it. And there are a variety of points at which
this connection needs to be particularly accentuated.
The first point is at the inception of the family life, when
the foundations of a new home are laid, when the marriage tie is knit. The state can only legalize marriages.
It is in the name of the ideal society, and its exalted
purposes, from which the new home receives the light
that is to fill it, that marriages are solemnized. Another
point of connection is to be found in the moral education of the young. If, indeed, a piece-meal morality is
not deemed sufficient; if it be desirable that the frag-
mentary virtues which are learned by casual precept and
example, be combined into a consistent scheme of conduct, then there must be offered to the minds of growing youths and maidens a distinct social ideal from which
all the several duties may be derived, in which they may
all be united, and which shall fill the young with a
noble enthusiasm for social service. The individualist is
mistaken if he believes that he can discharge this delicate pedagogical duty. An institution is needed to
provide for the satisfaction of this need. And again,
in the hour of bereavement, the family realizes its de-
pendence on the larger human society by which it is
enveloped. When the common fate has struck us, and
we relalize in our own case the common lot, it is only
the thought of the common purpose of mankind's existence on earth that can sustain us. It is Humanity, the

bearer of age-long sorrows, acquainted with nameless griefs ; humanity with its tear-stained face, with its scars and wounds, and yet also with the radiant eye that looks beyond and beyond, and its sad, wise smile of patience and resignation, that alone can hush our private griefs ! And it is this voice, through whatever mouth-piece, that should be heard in the house of mourning. To solemnize marriages, to whisper the reconciling words into the silence of death, to give point and unity to the moral life of the youg—these are some of the services to be expected from such societies as this. It is not good for families to stand alone, if they would have the best family life. Nor does the loose association of a group of friendly families, changeful, dependent, often, on mere accident, interest, or sentiment, supply the need. It is requisite that the family should not only be imbedded in the community, but organically related to it, and that through the medium of an ˙association, which has in it an element of permanence and greatness, because it stands for what is most lasting and greatest in the in-terests of society at large.

But our association has a duty to perform for the in-dividuals, as well as for the families, of which it is com-posed. There is a vessel of purest gold, says the Bud-dhist story, for which, when the Buddha saw it, he gave all that he had in exchange ; and then ran swiftly to the river's brink and plunged into the flood, risking his life in the attempt to save his treasure from those who would have robbed him of it. There is a pearl of great price, says the parable of the New Testament, for which the merchant who sought goodly pearls sold all his posses-sions in order that he might purchase it. There is one

thing needful—yes, for us, too—one thing needful. We
want a new doctrine of life to take the place of the disin-
tegrating creeds. We want to lay our hands upon the
sovereign throne of truth, even if the figure that sits
thereon be veiled. We want to come into touch with
the ultimate power in things, the ultimate peace in things,
which yet, in any literal sense, we know well that we
cannot know. We want to be morally certain ; that is,
certain for moral purposes of what is beyond the reach
of demonstration. Agnosticism, in the absolute sense,
does not exist. The strictest constructionist of the
limits of knowledge does yet plant certain stupendous
affirmations in the realm of the unknowable, certain
postulates—such as that of the uniformity of nature's
processes—the truth of which he can never fully verify,
which serve him rather as instruments for discovering
truths which he can verify. So we, too, are justified in
planting in the realm of the unknowable the working
hypothesis of human conduct, a postulate upon which
we depend in order to extend the boundaries and promote the ends of the good. And the postulate I have
in mind is identical with what is commonly called moral
optimism—the belief, namely, that the better side of
things will come uppermost ; that moral progress is not
a chimera ; that the course of evolution is not circular
but ascending ; that something worth while is developing in the world ; that the labor and the anguish are
not in vain ; that the good and the true are rooted in
the nature of things, and mingle their spurs in the sub-
soil of the universe. But this moral optimism, which
includes the darkest facts that pessimism can oppose—
includes and transcends them—how can we obtain it ?

To this question the answer is given in our name—
" Ethical Culture."

Of Goethe Carlyle said that " in his creations is embodied the religious wisdom which is proper to this
time, which may still reveal to us glimpses of the unseen
but not unreal world, that so clear knowledge may
be again wedded to religion." If Goethe had uttered
the religious teaching proper to this time, why have not
the multitudes fed on him and satisfied themselves with
his teachings ? Goethe, it is true, more than any one
else, inaugurated what is called the era of " culture."
But he was poet and artist, and his scheme of culture is
suited mainly for poets and artists like himself. The
rest of mankind it is calculated to satisfy only on one
side of their nature—the æsthetic side. To live earnestly, so as to produce genuine works of art ; to enter
into the deeper understanding of art, so as to give to
actual life the formal poise and finish of a work of art ;
in other words, to make harmony and beauty the beginning and the end of all human endeavor—such is the
gospel of culture as put forth by Goethe. · It is a gospel
the value of which as an element of wisdom cannot be
denied ; but it cannot, on the other hand, be said that it
is " the religious teaching which is proper to our time."
It is fitted for those who dwell on Olympian levels, not
for the dust-covered fighters in the arena ; for those who
stand aloof from the dire struggle for existence as spec-
tators, not for those who are subject to its stress and
strain. The watchword " culture " we may indeed
adopt. But there is needed the qualifying prefix " ethical " to give it a practical direction, and a still higher
aim than the æsthetic one. Culture, therefore, we also

say, but Ethical Culture ; and by that we mean that we
must appeal, not primarily to the feelings, as Goethe
did, but to the will ; that we shall seek the truest development of self, not in subjective enjoyment, however
subtle and refined, but in laboring for an objective
good ; that we shall ever be willing, if need be, to sacrifice the present harmony of our lives for the sake of a
far-off universal harmony which is to be in the future,
of which we can only dimly, faintly, foresee the beauty
and the holiness.   None the less, in weighty words, has
Goethe outlined the *method* of all culture, and that
method prescribes the cardinal rule which we, too, must
follow.   Words, he says, are incapable of articulating
what is best, and where words fail, the act, the deed,
clarifies.   Deeds, executive efforts, are the means which
put us in possession of the principles that should
underlie doing.   And this is also our persuasion ; and
hence the strenuous emphasis which we put on deeds
—not, as has been superficially understood, as if we
recommended what is called " the doing of good"—the
feeding of the hungry, the nursing of the sick, the edu-
coting of the ignorant—as a makeshift substitute to
console us in the despair of principles ; as a narcotic to
allay the pain which is caused by the absence of a great
central conviction—but deeds as the means of discovering principles, as a means of bringing to the birth a
truer, broader, and deeper conviction.

To such deeds we are challenged by the circumstances of the age in which we live.   This age is an
age of pleasure for the giddy, an age of anxiety and
profound concern for the thoughtful.   The murmuring
discontent that arises from the laboring masses, the

dangers that menace the institution of the family in
every civilized country, the failure that has attended
every experiment in democratic government thus far to
achieve the true welfare of nations, have raised a series
of terrifying problems which, sooner or later—and better
soon than late—society must meet. And all these
problems, as has been justly said, lead down, if we
follow them far enough, to ethical foundations, and.
depend for their solution upon two factors : a new
influx of moral power, and the evolution of a new conscience—that is, the clearer perception of those moral
requirements on which, amid the altered conditions of
the present, the progress of mankind depends. To aid
in the evolution of this new conscience, to inject living
streams of moral force into the dry veins of materialistic
communities, that was our program twenty years ago
when we began. That, seen in sharper outlines, is our
program to-day.

To you, members of my Society, who have accepted
this program ; who have, during so long a period, amid
manifold discouragements and against the odds of prejudice and misconstruction, sustained my own incip-
ient efforts in this great contention, whose loyalty and
trust have been to me perpetual springs of strength, I
owe, on this occasion, what ?—the expression of my personal sense of appreciation ? No, you do not expect that,
and I cannot offer it. What is best cannot articulate itself
in words ; and the ties that exist between us are too
intimate and delicate to become matter of formal recognition. Let us, rather, to-night jointly renew our oath
of allegiance to our flag. Let us consecrate ourselves,
with a more earnest purpose, to the work that is waiting

to be done.   And let us take heart of hope in the belief that the bells on the great watch-tower of time, as they ring out the passing years, will ring in, at last, the better day.   Ring out the old and in the new !   Ring out the false and in the true !

> '' Ring in the valiant man and free,
> The larger heart, the kindlier hand.
> Ring out the darkness of the land,
> Ring in the light that is to be ! ''

HISTORICAL SKETCHES OF ETHICAL SOCIETIES.

The Society for Ethical Culture of New York.

In the Centennial year of our national independence, when a general spirit of hopefulness was in the air, and the recollection of great events in the past stirred men's hearts, the corner-stone of the Society for Ethical Culture was laid. Even at that time the number of "liberal" societies in the country was considerable, and the teachings of men like Channing, Parker, and, above all, Emerson had done much to prepare the way for an Ethical Movement. On the 15th of May, 1876, several hundred persons, interested in the formation of a Society for Ethical Culture, met in Standard Hall, at the corner of Forty-second street and Broadway. Dr. Adler, then lecturer at Cornell University, delivered an address in which he gave expression to those principles on which the work of the Society has ever since rested. At the conclusion of the address the Society was regularly constituted. Thus the 15th of May became the birthday not only of the Ethical Society in New York, but of the Movement in America. The address of that evening is elsewhere reprinted in full.

The Sunday lectures were at first given in Standard Hall. After a few years, however, the accommodations proving insufficient, the Society removed to Chickering Hall, where it remained until 1892. The audiences having again outgrown the capacity of the Hall, another change became necessary, and during the past four years the lectures have been delivered in the Carnegie Music hall, at the corner of Fifty-seventh street and Seventh avenue. The work of the Society has always attracted much attention outside of its own membership. About half the seats in the large hall are reserved for strangers, and many thousands have availed themselves of this privilege and come under the

(35)

influence of the Movement, even if they have not directly allied themselves with it. Very early in the history of the Society a number of young men were attracted to the ideas which it represented and prepared themselves to undertake the duties of Ethical leadership. After remaining a few years in New York with Prof. Adler, one after another of these men went out to found new Societies in different cities of the United States. Thirteen years ago Mr. W. M. Salter became lecturer of the Ethical Society in Chicago.* Two years later another Society was founded in Philadelphia, under the direction of Mr. S. Burns Weston. A fourth was established in St. Louis, just ten years ago, by Mr. W. L. Sheldon. Dr. Stanton Coit, who had also been lecturer in New York for several years, found a congenial field of work in England, and established the West London Ethical Society ; while in Germany, in Austria, in Italy and in Switzerland the same Movement has recently taken root. The following sketch of the various educational and philanthropic activities in which the New York Society is engaged will best show in what way the life of the Society is expressing itself.

THE ETHICAL CULTURE SCHOOLS.

If Ethical Culture is to become a reality, it must be begun among the young and then continued unremittingly in manhood and old age. The moral development of children is promoted to some extent by direct moral instruction, but it depends even in a greater degree upon a thousand subtle moral influences. The home is usually regarded as the place where the child is to be surrounded by such influences. But the daily school also affords the most valuable opportunities for the same sort of influence, and its importance in this connection is not generally recognized as much as it ought to be. If the Ethical Culture Movement is to be perpetuated, it must get hold of the young. If it is to get hold of the young, it must gain possession of the daily school. The New York Society, starting from this conviction, undertook to establish a school of its own, which has steadily grown and which now numbers over four hundred pupils. This school has,

---

* Of which the present leader is Mr. M. M. Mangasarian, Mr. Salter having taken charge of the Society in Philadelphia

in many ways, marked a new departure. It was the first to introduce manual training as a regular part of the curriculum in all classes. The teaching of art and elementary science received particular attention. A system of unsectarian moral instruction was introduced, the aim of which was to demonstrate practically how ethical ideas might be conveyed to the minds of children independently of theological dogmas. The methods of the school have been widely studied, commented on, and partly copied in this and other countries. But what is characteristic of this institution is its spirit rather than its technique. As illustrative of this spirit the following points may be mentioned :

First, the greatest possible pains are taken by the staff of teachers to discover the bent of every pupil and to develop him along the lines of his natural aptitude, on the principle that every human being that is born into the world is unique to some extent, however slightly, and that his "salvation" consists in being helped to express what he was designed by nature to be. The art, science, technical skill, literary training, etc., employed in this school, besides subserving the purposes of elementary culture in general, are more specifically applied as so many tests for ascertaining the individual bent of the pupils.

Secondly, a school diary is kept, in which the characteristic qualities of the child—intellectual and moral—as they show themselves, are noted down. This record is carefully continued from the day the child enters the school until it leaves. Its intellectual and moral development is thus, as far as possible, photographed, with the design of helping the teachers and parents more thoroughly to understand the child—its needs, its virtues, its defects, the promise which it seems to contain, the peculiar perils by which it seems to be menaced.

Thirdly, every effort is made to create in the school an enthusiasm for social service. Labor is the central idea to which all other ideas are correlated—labor in the interest of the progress of mankind. The story of human civilization is told as far as children are able to understand it. The inter-dependence of the various occupations and vocations is explained in the same way. The lives of the great thinkers and doers who have led the race forward on its path are held up for admiration. The school considers its task accomplished if its pupils go forth carrying with them the idea of efficient and thorough work, with scorn in their hearts for slipshod performance of any sort, and with the earnest desire to render some kind of service to humanity according to the measure of their ability.

Lastly, it may be stated that the school can never degenerate into a class school—a rule of the Board of Trustees requiring that at least fifty per cent. of the pupils shall be the children of poor parents. The mingling of social classes—the democratic constitution of the school—is regarded as an important factor in developing character and creating a right view of life.

The school at present takes pupils up to the fourteenth year. A system of secondary schools is being planned, and has already been started, which is intended to carry the work of the society up to the beginnings of manhood and womanhood.

THE WORK OF THE YOUNG MEN.

Early in the history of the Society there was formed a group of young men, known as the "Union for the Higher Life." This little Union was productive of excellent results. There was a tacit understanding among the members as to certain matters relating to the conduct of life—for instance, as to purity and charity. The members taxed themselves strictly for purposes of charity (the main point being that charity should be regarded as a duty, and not be left to mere impulse), and further, they were to make it their aim to increase in ethical knowledge and insight. The little Union has furnished to the Society some of its most faithful members and most earnest workers. For a long time it supported a home for neglected children ; and this home was only discontinued after its inmates had become self-supporting. It is hoped that the Union will be renewed and enlarged during the coming winter.

Under the leadership of Dr. John Elliott, and with the assistance of the young men of the Society, an attempt is being made to disseminate the moral ideas for which the Society stands among the inhabitants of one of the poorest tenement-house districts of New York. A number of clubs for workingmen and boys have been formed for this purpose, the good influence of which is

already beginning to be felt in the neighborhood. The immediate object of these clubs is to redeem those who belong to them
from the half-savage life of the streets, to promote social refinement, to create a taste for good literature, to stimulate the slug-
gish mind, and to awaken higher and better aspirations.

The Young Men's Union, so-called, an association consisting
of several hundred members, contributes to the social life of the
Ethical Society by a series of monthly entertainments, and has
been highly useful in furnishing financial aid toward the charities
of the Society.

The Young People's Union of Harlem is engaged in the serious study of ethical and social questions, under the leadership of
the best teachers to be found on these subject.*

THE WORK OF THE WOMEN.

In the Spring of 1893 the Women's Conference of the Society
for Ethical Culture was organized. The various groups of women
working within the general lines of the Women's Conference are:

1. The Ladies' Auxiliary Union, founded fifteen years ago,
with a present membership of 150. The object of this group is
to supply garments and other necessaries for the sick to various
hospitals and dispensaries, and indirectly to assist a number of
deserving women in earning a decent livelihood.

2. The Ladies' Committee of the United Relief Works, the
object of which is to assure a certain sum every year to the man-
agers of the charities of the Society. This Committee has done
most efficient work, and has usually raised a sum equal to about
one-fourth of the Society's current expenses for charity.

3. The Visiting and Teaching Guild for Crippled Children.
This Guild has been in existence for seven years. Its object is
to visit crippled children in their homes, to bring to them the
education which they are debarred, by their infirmity, from obtaining at school, to cheer and comfort them during the months,
and often years, of confinement to which they are subject.

4. The Mothers' Society for the Study of Child Nature. This

---

* "The Fortnightly," like the Young People's Union, is devoted to the study of
ethical and social questions, with the difference, however, that the discussions are less
formal, the subjects being discussed by the members themselves, without the assistance
of expert leaders.

has existed for eight years. Its object is to familiarize mothers with the best educational literature, with the works of Locke, Rousseau, Pestalozzi, Froebel, etc., and to prepare them to deal intelligently and sensitively with the educational problems that arise in their own homes.

5. The Wage Earners' Section of the Ethical Culture Society. The object of this Section is to provide for the women wage-earners, who are members of the Society, special means of intellectual culture, to stimulate among them a deeper interest in the so-called labor question, and to assist in practical efforts at improving the condition of female wage-earners.

Other work of the women of the Society: During the severe distress of the Winter of 1893 relief work-shops were organized by a Committee of the Women's Conference, acting in conjunction with a Committee of the Young Men's Union, for the assistance of the unemployed. The sum of $17,000 was raised and hundreds of women were supplied with temporary work sufficient to keep them above starvation. A number of the members of the Women's Conference have also taken a special interest in the formation of a Children's Guild. The aim of this Guild, which was begun in March, 1895, is to unite the children of the Society in a fellowship for good work, and to bring them early into touch with the philanthrophic activities of the Society to which they belong. There are about 125 children enrolled in this Guild, and the income derived from the contributions of the young members is used to support a number of afternoon classes for children in one of the poorer districts of New York. The object of the classes is to furnish both entertainment and instruction in such branches as are more or less neglected in the public schools.

Besides the practical activities referred to, the Women's Conference seeks to discuss and define woman's true position in the state, in industry, in science and art, and in the home. For this purpose monthly lectures are delivered in which the problems involved are considered on the highest plane.

THE SUNDAY ETHICAL CLASSES.

Of these they are six, attended by over 150 pupils. It has already been stated that moral instruction can best be given in the daily school. The seggregation of this branch of teaching into a so-called Sunday-school is a mere makeshift. The whole atmosphere of the daily school should be charged with moral ozone. All the influences that play upon the child should make for character. The object of the moral lesson should be neither more nor less than to fix, develop and clarify habits and sentiments and ideas which the child has, so to speak, already absorbed at every pore. The assemblies of the children on Sunday should have the same purpose as the Sunday meetings of their elders. Their object should be to inspire and edify. And as a considerable number of the children of the members of our Society do not attend our daily school, it has been found necessary to combine in our Sunday children's meetings the two objects of teaching and edification. The work of teaching is conducted, in the main, along the lines marked out in Dr. Adler's book on "The Moral Instruction of Children." The second object is sought to be attained by exercises in which all the class join, consisting of singing, a brief responsorium, and an address by the superintendent or one of the teachers in which an appeal is made to the spiritual nature of the young.

Ethical classes are also conducted on week-days, in the afternoon or evening, for advanced pupils, in which instruction is given in religious history, and in which the special duties pertaining to the life of young men and young women are considered.

GENERAL CHARITIES OF THE SOCIETY.

Among these, one of the oldest and one of the most beneficent is the District Nursing System, which was begun by the Ethical Culture Society in 1868, and has been widely imitated in New York and elsewhere. Trained nurses are sent into the homes of the poor to give them skilled attendance in sickness, to relieve pain and to provide conditions favorable for recovery ; and also to bring the civilizing influence of gentleness, patience and refinement into these often squalid and degraded homes. That the nurse must be a lady in the best sense is an indispensable condition. Many thousands of sufferers have been reached in this way. Many a life, we are led to believe, has been saved, and seeds of good have been disseminated which are not likely to be wholly wasted.

MATTERS EXTERNAL.

The number of enrolled members of the New York Society is, at present, about 800. As many of these are heads of families, the actual number of persons affiliated with the Society is much larger. The educational and charitable work is chiefly carried on under the auspices of the United Relief Works, an association which has a legal existence of its own distinct from that of the Society for Ethical Culture. But the two associations are identical in spirit and purpose; the principal workers are the same, and the circle from which their support is derived is largely, if not entirely, the same. It is fair, therefore, in speaking of their resources, to class them together. The annual budget of the Society for the maintenance of its platform and its charities amounts to something over $50,000. Of this $20,000 goes to the Society proper; $30,000 to the charities. The Society possesses a sinking fund of between $60,000 and $70,000. The United Relief Works own the building at 109 West Fifty-fourth street, in which the school is carried on. In addition, the sum of $100,000 has already been subscribed toward the erection of a new and spacious edifice, in which it is proposed that all the various activities of the Society shall be united. The further prosecution of this much-needed enterprise has been checked by the financial depression which has visited the United States during the past few years. But, with a return of prosperity, it is earnestly hoped that the plan, which is suspended for the moment, will be taken up with new vigor, and that the Society will secure a home worthy of the place which it now occupies in the community, giving free room for the expansion of those energies which are, at present, cramped and impeded.

The Chicago Ethical Society.

The impulse to the formation of the Society for Ethical Culture of Chicago was given by addresses on "The True Method of Religious Reform" and "Do the Ethics of Jesus Satisfy the Needs of Our Time?" by Prof. Felix Adler and Mr. W. M.

Salter respectively, in the Grand Opera House, Sunday afternoon, October 1st, 1882. Mr. Salter was called the following spring to the lectureship of the Society and gave his opening lecture (on "The Basis of the Ethical Movement") on Sunday morning, April 1st, to about sixty-five people, in Hershey Music Hall. On the following Sunday a Children's Ethical Class was started with three members. A Normal Class was formed for the training of future teachers of Ethical Classes. Steps were also taken to form the Relief Works, which initiated District Nursing for the benefit of the sick poor in Chicago, as the Relief Works of the parent Society had done in New York. (The latter work gradually extended itself, but was discontinued after two years, on account of the lack of co-operation of the dispensaries from which the nurses received their cases.)

In 1884–5 the Sunday lectures were held in Weber Music Hall. The two following years the Society met in Hershey Music Hall. In the autumn of 1887 it moved to the Grand Opera House, where it has continued ever since. In the main the Society's work prospered. A Ladies' Charitable Union was formed, also a Young People's Union, and a Young Men's Club for the study of Philosophy and Social Ethics. Permanent headquarters were secured for week-day meetings, known as Emerson Hall. The one small Children's Class became an Ethical School of sixty members. The Sunday audiences came to average two hundred and fifty. Reading Circles were started on the three sides of the city and studied in particular the history of the French Revolution. Individual members started enterprises of public benefit, such as the "Economic Conferences between Business Men and Workingmen," and the "Bureau of Justice," and joined in the agitation of questions of popular justice (such as the Eight-Hour Question and the execution of the "Anarchists"). Ill health compelled the resignation of Mr. Salter and his removal to a milder climate, after nearly nine years of service—though not without having secured an assurance of the willingness of Mr. M. M. Mangasarian to be his successor.

Mr. Mangasarian gave his opening lecture (on "The New Ethical Preacher") February 7th, 1892. The Sunday audiences at the Grand Opera House to listen to his lectures usually fill the house to its utmost capacity, and the lectures are frequently well reported in the press of the city and neighboring towns.

Regular quarterly meetings are held, at which the members discuss matters of general interest to the Society and transact such business as is required, after which the remainder of the evening is given to social intercourse.

The Social Union is designed to encourage social intercourse among the members, and to this end literary and musical entertainments are often provided.

The active work of the Society is under the charge of special committees.

Five young men have charge of the publications, and distribute the literature of the movement at the Sunday meetings.

The Economic Section is an outgrowth of the Adult Class of the Sunday Ethical School. At the close of the lecture season in 1894 the class decided to continue its meetings during the summer, studying social conditions and discussing current social, political and economic questions. Addresses were made by the young men and women of the class, and the attendance continually increased. Many new members were brought into the Society through these meetings. In the autumn of that year the Economic Section was regularly organized and meetings were held on Sunday evenings, prominent persons in local public life being invited to speak. Among those who addressed the meetings were Miss Jane Addams, Mr. Henry D. Lloyd, Mr. Hamlin Garland, Mr. J. Keir Hardie of Scotland, Prof. E. W. Bemis, Rev. Carlous Martyn, Judge Lorin C. Collins, Mr. Thomas J. Morgan, Mr. William Hope Harvey (Coin's Financial School), Mr. William M. Salter, and many others. The aim of this Section is expressed in the words of Prof. Adler, printed at the head of each program, "Be it ours to lift the fallen, to lend free utterance to the complaints of the oppressed, to brand the social iniquities of our time, and to give our hearts' warmth and the labor of our hands to the cause of their redress." The Economic Section is already a recognized influence in the city.

The Ladies' Union is organized to prepare garments for the sick poor and maintain a visiting nurse.

The Sunday Ethical School, which has always been a prominent feature of the Society, follows a course of study that has been gradually developed and has some features that originated in Chicago. Prof. Adler's "The Moral Instruction of Children" has been found helpful in perfecting the course. The School is divided into eight grades. The children of the first grade (during most of the year divided into two classes) are taught by means of fables and fairy tales. The second grade, composed of children eight or nine years of age, have selected stories from the Old Testament. ⋅ The Greek heroes and Homer furnish the material for the work of the third grade. The pupils of the next year have been taking up the "Beginnings" of the earth, of animals and plants, of mankind, of society, religions, etc. Selected biographies have been the subject of the work of the fifth grade. In the sixth year the pupils take up systematically a study of the various duties of life. The two higher classes have been studying the lives of the great religious and moral teachers, one class spending the entire year on the life of Jesus, the other dividing the time between Buddha and Socrates. The enrollment of the different classes varies from six or seven to nearly twenty. Many of the pupils come long distances—those from several families as far as eight miles. The School is opened by twenty or thirty minutes of singing, under the direction of a skillful leader, accompanied by a short talk from the superintendent or a stanza of verse repeated by one of the children.

The Philadelphia Ethical Society.

The Society for Ethical Culture of Philadelphia was organized June 1st, 1885. The circumstances which led to the organization of the Philadelphia Society were briefly as follows : During the winter 1884-5 Mr. S. Burns Weston, then studying and working with Professor Adler in New York, visited Philadelphia to see whether an Ethical Society could be organized there. A few persons interested in the project arranged a course of six lectures, to be given on Sunday mornings in the spring of 1885, explaining the ideas and aims of the Ethical Movement. The course was opened April 5th, the first four lectures being given by

Mr. Weston, the fifth by Mr. William M. Salter—at that time the lecturer for the Society for Ethical Culture of Chicago—and the closing lecture by Prof. Felix Adler. This resulted in twenty-four persons coming together on June 1st and organizing themselves into "The Society for Ethical Culture of Philadelphia."

The Society started out with having women represented on its Board of Trustees, a policy which it has adhered to ever since. The Constitution and Statement of Principles provided for the formation of Sections of various kinds for the study, discussion and application of ethical principles in the special departments of life which each section should represent. The Constitution also provided that at least one-fourth of the entire income of the Society should be devoted to philanthropic work. The minimum annual membership dues were fixed at ten dollars.

The regular public work began Sunday, October 18th, 1885, at Natatorium Hall, with a lecture by Professor Adler and a short address by Mr. Weston, who had been invited to become the lecturer of the Society. A Children's Ethical Class was immediately started, and also a Business Men's Section for the study of business ethics, a Household Section to study the economics and the ethics of the home, and a Young Men's Section to discuss questions of special interest to young men. The Section meetings were held regularly and gave rise to many interesting papers and discussions by the members.

Only a few weeks after the active work of the Society began a number of newsboys and bootblacks, found on the street near Natatorium Hall, were organized (November, 1885) into a Boys' Club, which met Sunday afternoons and week-day evenings, various kinds of amusements and instruction being provided. The Club increased in size, a larger place was rented, new features were added, and the work was carried successfully along for a year or two under the direct auspices of the Society. In order, however, to carry on the work on a much larger scale, it was finally decided to hand it over to a new organization, called the Neighborhood Guild Association, composed of prominent citizens outside of the Society, whom the lecturer had invited to come together for this purpose. The Boys' Club was then merged into a "Neighborhood Guild," a name simultaneously chosen in New

York and Philadelphia for this kind of social work among the children of the poor in the two cities. Under the auspices of the Neighborhood Guild Association the work assumed larger proportions and was carried on successfully for several years, when it was finally merged into other similar organizations.

During the first year of the Philadelphia Society steps were also taken to organize a day-school with an educational system similar to that of the Workingman's School of New York. "The Ethical School," as it was called, was opened with a kindergarten and the common school branches in the autumn of 1886, in a central location, a house having been rented for that purpose. A branch school was soon started in West Philadelphia. The teaching in both schools was of a high grade from the first and in accordance with the most advanced methods. For two or three years both schools were continued under the auspices of the Society, when the central school, not being self-supporting but making large financial demands on the Society, had to be discontinued. The West Philadelphia Branch was self-support-ing almost from the first and has had a successful history, being still in a prosperous condition. It is no longer, however, under the auspices of the Ethical Society, its entire control.having been handed over three or four years ago to the able principal who has been at its head almost from the beginning, and who, it may be added, is a member of the Ethical Society.

In May, 1890, Mr. Weston resigned the lectureship of the Society, after having been its lecturer for five years. For the first four years the lectures were held in Natatorium Hall, on South Broad street, and after that in St. George's Hall, on Arch street, where they were continued until the autumn of 1892, since which time they have been held in New Century Hall, 124 South Twelfth street.

After Mr. Weston's resignation the Society was without a lecturer for about a year and a half, during which time various people were invited to occupy the platform from Sunday to Sunday. One miscellaneous section continued weekly meetings and an adult class met for an hour before the Sunday morning lecture. At this time the Constitution and By-laws were entirely revised and the clause in regard to minimum annual dues of ten dollars was abolished, each one being expected to contribute according to his ability. In place of the long Statement of Principles, drawn up when the Society was organized, this brief statement (taken from the Constitution of the American Ethical Union) was adopted :

"The General Aim of the Society for Ethical Culture of Philadelphia is the elevation of the moral life of its members and that of the community, and it welcomes to its fellowship all who sympathize with this aim, whatever may be their theological or philosophical opinions."

In February, 1892, Mr. William M. Salter, formerly the lecturer of the Chicago Society, assumed the lectureship of the Philadelphia Society. Under his leadership the Society has grown steadily stronger internally, and a hundred and seventy-one new members have joined.

The Section work has been entirely reorganized and extended, and its various meetings are now an important feature of the Society's work. There are at present the following Sections : Reform Section, Economic Section, Literature and Art Section, Philosophical Section, and a Women's Section. There is also a Young People's Club and a Young Men's Union. The Reform Section was organized for practical work, and its first efforts have been directed towards forming a consumers' League, and it is also interesting itself in forming unions among the working women and girls of Philadelphia.

In the Sunday Ethical School the Adult Classes continue as before, and there are now five other classes studying respectively Politics, Greek Literature, Personal Duties, Fables, and Fairy Tales and Nature Lessons. The Ethical School was never in so good a condition.

The Society has had three hundred and fifty-six names enrolled on its membership list since it was organized. Owing to a controversy in 1894, which involved the issue as to whether the Society had any moral standard or was simply a Society for ethical study and discussion, twenty-six members withdrew after the annual meeting of that year.

For the past two years the Society has had rooms at 1305 Arch street, where an Ethical Library and Reading Room has been started, which is open to the general public at stated hours.

In 1888 the Philadelphia Society began the publication of the first official organ of the Societies for Ethical Culture, a quarterly, called *The Ethical Record*. The publication was continued for two years and a half, when it was succeeded, in October, 1890, by the *International Journal of Ethics*, which, though not the official organ of the Ethical Societies, owes its origin and main support to them. The publication of *Ethical Addresses*, issued monthly with the exception of July and August, was begun in January, 1894.

In January, 1895, Mr. Salter began a monthly publication, *The Cause*, which is " Devoted to Moral Progress and the Interests of the Society for Ethical Culture of Philadeldhia." This is an eight page publication, which, besides giving a full account of the work going on in the Philadelphia Society, contains interesting reports of the progress of the movement in other places. It is distributed free at the Sunday meetings of the Society, and is manily supported by voluntary contributions.

Mr. Salter organized, in January, 1895, an Ethical Society in Kensington, an extensive manufacturing district in the northeast of Philadelphia. Meetings have been regularly held during the lecture season on Sunday evenings, and are attended for the most part by workingmen.

The St. Louis Ethical Society.

In the spring of 1886 Mr. Sheldon was invited by a committee to give a course of three lectures in the hall connected with the Museum of Fine Arts. This was the beginning which led to the organization of the Society the ensuing fall when Mr. Sheldon was chosen lecturer, a position which he has now held for ten years. Every season there has been a regular series of lectures given at Memorial Hall. An effort has been made to enlist all classes of people in the great ethical problems of the day, and educational work along ethical lines has been started in different parts of the city. The Society is therefore in part supported by persons who value it for the good it does for St. Louis. It has been in a way like an " Ethical Institute " for the city.

Among those who have spoken on Sunday morning at Memorial Hall, besides the regular lecturer, have been several leading educators of the United States or men occupying professional chairs at the various universities, such as Prof. Josiah Royce and Prof. F. Taussig of Harvard University, Prof. Paul Shorey and Prof. J. Lawrence Laughlin of the University of Chicago, as well as all the lecturers of the other Ethical Societies.

The most important practical educational work started by the Society in St. Louis has been a movement for providing opportunities for general self-culture among workingmen and their families.   The first step taken was to open some free reading rooms. Then a course of lectures was given on Friday evenings.   The movement spread elsewhere in St. Louis, and a second branch was opened on the South Side of the city.   A year or two ago a third branch was started in a new manufacturing center known as Tower Grove.   The basis of this educational work was to be the principle of strict neutrality on matters pertaining to religion. This institution has been steadily advancing until it now occupies two entire buildings in different portions of the city.   Five lecture courses are going on every week, with classes in "Cooking," "Dressmaking," "Civil Government," "Elocution," "Literature" and other subjects.   Those who attend are members of the "young men's clubs" and "young women's clubs," each of which has its separate lecture courses.

Some of the lectures are arranged in series.   For instance, there has been one course on "Natural Science," a second on "Architecture," a third on "Biographies of great Men," and a fourth on "Biographies of great Women."   Nearly all of the leading educators of the city have co-operated in this work : there having been seventy or eighty different lecturers last season, including eight or ten of the leading clergymen of the city, from the Baptist, Methodist, Presbyterian, Episcopal, Unitarian and Jewish churches, and also about an equal number of the foremost lawyers of the city, including Gen. John W. Noble, who was Secretary of the Interior under President Harrison ; several of the leading business men of the city, a number of the leading physicians, several of the professors of the Washington University, ten or twelve members of the Wednesday Club, a member of Congress from this city, and others. The attendance is usually very good. The clubs are known as "Wage-Earners' Self-Culture Clubs."

One conspicuous feature in this undertaking has been what is known as "Domestic Economy Schools." They are intended to teach young girls the elements of knowledge essential in the care of a home. These classes meet on Saturday forenoon and afternoon and have been remarkably successful.

This branch of work, including the "Domestic Economy Schools" and the "Wage-Earners' Self-Culture Clubs," became so important that it was finally separated from the Ethical Society and made an independent corporation, the only connection with the Society being that the lecturer still has general charge of the educational work of this institution. He has, however, an assistant, who resides at one of the Self-Culture Halls and devotes nearly all of his time to the work. The Domestic Economy Schools have been developed through the devoted efforts of a corps of ladies interested in this special phase of education.

Another interesting educational effort on the part of the Ethical Society has been a series of courses of "Sunday Afternoon Popular Science Lectures," given at one of the down-town theaters during the winter months, or at the entertainment hall of the Exposition Building. The first series was given by residents of St. Louis. The last two years the lectures have been given by eminent scientists from other parts of the United States. Professor E. D. Cope of the University of Pennsylvania, gave one on "Fishes;" Prof. F. M. Chapman of the American Academy of Natural Sciences, gave one on "Birds;" Prof. L. O. Howard, of the Smithsonian Institution at Washington, one on "Insects;" Prof. Angelo Heilprin has given one on "Ice and Glaciers" and another on "Explorations in the Arctic Regions." A small admission fee was charged at these lectures which has just covered the expenses. The attendance has been usually quite large, ranging from six hundred to one thousand people at nearly every lecture.

The Ethical Society has also tried to start general educational work in special sections of St. Louis, where such work seems to be neglected. During the last two years courses of lectures have been given in North St. Louis on "American History" by professors of the Washington University; also by several other leading educators of the city.   On the other hand, there has been active work for educational purposes on subjects directly ethical in character.   Five years ago a club was organized among the women of the city for the purpose of studying "Applied Ethics," taking up the work historically.   They began the first year with a study of "Greek Ethics."   The second year was devoted to the "Ethics of Rome;" the third year to the "Renaissance;" the fourth year to the "Seventeenth and Eighteenth Centuries;" and this last season has been given to a study of the "Modern Poets."   While the club has been directly in charge of the Ethical Society, it has been attended by people of the most widely divergent views.   Roman Catholics, Presbyterians, Unitarians, etc. attend the meetings and join in the discussions.   The name of the organization was taken from the first year's work.   It has therefore been known as the "Greek Ethics Club."

Another educational work was organized for young men to meet fortnightly Wednesday evenings—being known as the "Political Science Club."   The intention was to encourage young men to study the problems of Social and Political Science instead of giving so much time to mere discussion.   They began founding a small library, getting the standard or classical works on these subjects, and subscribing for the leading quarterlies.   The first year they had a course of lectures on "Political Economy;" the second year a series of talks on the "Duties of Public Officers."   "The work of a State Governor" was described by a recent Governor of Missouri.   "The work of a Cabinet Officer" was described by a member of the Cabinet under President Harrison.   The Mayor of St. Louis gave a talk on the "Duties and Work of a City Mayor."   Another talk was on the "Work of a Minister to a Foreign Country," by a citizen of St. Louis, who had been Minister of the United States to Switzerland.   They have also had a series of talks on Commercial Institutions.   A description of a "Board of Trade" was given by a former president of the Merchants' Exchange of St. Louis.   The "Banking System" was described by a prominent banker of the city.   "A Great City Post Office" was portrayed by the City Postmaster.

They have also had three talks on the "Supreme Court of the United States," by one of the foremost lawyers of the West.

The Ethical Society has Children's Classes, meeting on Sunday morning, similar to those held in other cities. At the close of ten years' work of the St. Louis Ethical Society an Ethical Congress was held, including also a Convention of all the Ethical Societies of America.

The Ethical Movement in Germany, Austria and Switzerland.

The most decisive impulse toward the formation of Ethical Societies in Germany was that given by the lectures of Prof. Adler in the spring of 1892, previous to which a stimulus in the same spirit had come from *Oberstleutenant* von Egidy. The translation and dissemination of the writings of Messrs. Salter, Adler and Coit by Prof. von Gizycki of the University of Berlin had also served to prepare the soil for the growth of the Ethical Movement.

The German Ethical Society was incorporated at Berlin in October, 1892, admitting five hundred members within a few months. At present the Society includes nine branches, so called, namely, those of Berlin, Breslau, Frankfort, Freiburg, Königsberg, Magdeburg, München, Strassburg and Ulm. There are also five smaller divisions at Karlsruhe, Kiel, Mühlhausen, Nauen and Nordhausen. Besides these, two larger Societies, at Leipzig and Jena, belong to the Movement, but owing to local conditions have not yet joined the larger organization. Thus there are sixteen Societies in the various parts of Germany. The Berlin branch, with four subdivisions, counts about nine hundred members. The others average each about ninety members ; Jena and Leipzig together about one hundred and fifty, so that the total membership of all the Ethical Societies in Germany at present may be estimated at about eighteen hundred.

The work of these Societies may be summed up as follows :

1. Mutual intellectual aid and stimulus by means of lectures and discussions on subjects of pedagogical, ethical and sociolog-ico-ethical interest.

2. The dissemination of literature on the same questions.

3. Arranging lectures and courses of lectures for the public, in order to give special prominence to ethical and political teachings.

4. Efforts to influence the press by means of letters on ethical subjects.

5. Collecting and classifying data and material concerning matters of jurisprudence and penology.

6. Establishing of bureaux to aid those who are in need of work, of advice or material aid, combined with study of statistics in the care of the poor.

7. Founding of free public libraries and reading rooms.

8. Increasing opportunities for all classes to enjoy art.

9. Co-operation in the settlement and arbitration of strikes.

Increase in the membership of the Societies as a rule is a matter of slow growth. Far more marked in its influence seem to be the resulting ethical discussion and treatment of pedagogical and social questions, as shown partly in the growth and increasing influence of its weekly organ—*Ethische Kultur*. This paper was started in 1893 by the chief founder of the Ethical Society, the late Prof. G. von Giyzcki of Germany. It is at present edited by Dr. F. W. Foerster.

In Austria the first Ethical Society was founded at Vienna in the beginning of 1895. The present membership is about three hundred. The work of the Society is similar to that of the German Society as detailed above.

In Switzerland the first Ethical Society was founded in the latter part of 1895. Its work is closely allied to that of the other Societies. Its membership is about eighty.

.

THE RECENT CONGRESS OF AMERI-CAN AND EUROPEAN ETHICAL SOCIETIES AT ZURICH.*

BY FELIX ADLER.

LIGHT is the symbol of life. There is ever a cheering quality in it, whether we see it in a landscape or in a room ; but there are occasions when the benignity of the light comes home to us with a peculiarly satisfying completeness. One such occasion is especially present in my mind at this moment: We have been traversing the sea ; we are about to emerge from the waste of waters ; we approach the land ; but the moment is an anxious one, for the night is dark and the coast is girt with dangerous reefs and rocks. Suddenly, as we peer into the darkness, a beacon light flashes ahead ; it shows but for a moment and disappears ; it waxes and then it wanes, and then as we get nearer it grows and grows until it seems to fill the eye, and through the eye the soul, with its flood of splendor. Ah, how we realize at such a moment the benignity of the light ! How grateful we are for the friendliness of man ! At great cost and often at the risk of life, have these watch-towers been placed on the fringes of continents to warn men of the dangers which they must avoid and to indicate the port of safety to which they must steer.

---

* An Address given at Carnegie Hall, New York, Sunday, Oct. 18, 1896.

So, too, in the moral world watch-towers have been erected to warn us of the dangers to be avoided and to indicate the port of safety to which we must steer. From of old Christianity and indeed all the religions of the past have been busy raising these towers; but many of them are crumbling into decay; and new rocks, new reefs, new points of danger have been discovered of which the religions of the past have never given us warning and which are now becoming the scene and the cause of frequent disaster. It is the purpose of the Ethical Movement to help to repair these crumbling towers and to place beacons on those dangerous rocks which have heretofore escaped notice. And that the importance of this purpose is being recognized not only in our own community but also abroad in foreign countries among persons who live in an environment totally different from ours, is a fact that marks a significant step in the advance of our cause. I wish to-day to report to you concerning the recent Congress of Ethical Societies at Zurich, in which this community of interest and of purpose became manifest despite great differences.

The countries represented at the Congress, besides the United States and England, were Germany, Austria, Italy and Switzerland. The conferences were preceded by courses of lectures on ethical subjects by eminent ethical professors; and at these lecture courses the French government was officially represented by two delegates, the Minister of Education having deputed them to report especially upon the degree to which the Ethical Societies have succeeded in devising a course of ethical instruction for children, a subject in which the French Republic has a notable interest.

Now Germany, of all these countries, is the one where the Ethical Movement has obtained, till now, the largest extension ; the number of societies is considerable ; they are planted in all the chief cities of the Empire. And this is all the more interesting when we remember that the entire movement in Europe is only four years old, apart from England. The fact that there are now these numerous societies in Germany, that there is at least one strong society in Vienna, and that, as I shall show you presently, the movement is spreading to Italy and Switzerland, indicates that there is something in the idea for which the Ethical Movement stands that appeals to people irrespective of nationality, irrespective of local conditions.

I should like first to say something about the preparation which existed in Germany for the reception of the idea for which this movement stands. Germany has been a very religious country. The German people have been profoundly susceptible to religious influence. The Protestant Reformation, as we all know, originated in Germany, and as late as the last century we find that the thinkers and the men of science were still on the side of positive religion. Even Kant, who shattered the traditional proofs of the existence of a Deity, nevertheless made a place in his system for the belief in a personal God. Now within a hundred years all this seems to have changed. A cold breath has swept over Germany. Intellect seems to be no longer on the side of faith. The highly educated class hold aloof. They are not actively antagonistic to religion—they are indifferent ; they no longer lend it their support. Outwardly, indeed, the churches maintain their preeminent position through

the favor of the government. The military authorities
show their respect for the prevailing opinions ; men who
take high rank in the various sciences now and then attend
divine service ; but it is felt that, on the whole, the sanction of the educated elite of the country is lacking. Of
course I do not mean to imply that Germany has ceased
to be a religious country. The masses, for instance, are
still very powerfully under the influence of religious traditions. I shall never forget a scene I witnessed four
years ago at Trève, when the so-called seamless coat
of Christ, which is exhibited once every fifty years,
was shown to the people. I shall never forget that
scene : the eager multitudes, especially the throng of
peasants that stood in the streets under the open
skies day and night, waiting for a chance to approach
the relic—singing, chanting, with their crosses, their
banners, and their priests leading them. I could not
help gathering the impression that religious fanaticism,
like a hot bed of coals, is slumbering under white ashes
and ready, perhaps, to start into a devouring flame at
the first breath, and to become all the more misguided
and dangerous because the participation of the educated
classes is missing.

When a country is thus divided into two classes,
when there is a gulf between the life of the educated
and the ignorant masses, both will suffer. The educated
come to be out of touch with the common life and the
people are left to their dense and dark superstition.

But educated Germany has not been without some
substitute for the religious impulse which during the
last hundred years it has largely lacked. A nation whose
emotional life is so profound and whose intellectual as-

pirations are so high does not easily resign itself to the loss of that elevation which comes from the pursuit of idealistic ends ; and so there have been substitutes for religion.   One of these substitutes has been the idealism of science.   I mean by this that exaltation which is brought into the life of the person who devotes himself to the pursuit of abstract truth for truth's sake, without reference to its utilitarian applications and without any thought of pecuniary gain for himself.   Of this priestly consecration to abstract truth modern Germany has offered many great examples.   And if man were purely an intellectual being, if he could withdraw into his intellectual shell and ignore the emotional and moral interests, this idealism of abstract truth might answer the purpose.   But man is not a purely intellectual being, and the longer you make the experiment of feeding him on a merely intellectual idealism the more will the other side of his nature, the practical and the emotional side, rebel, rise in mutiny and press its claims.   And as science has very little to offer man on the emotional side, as the theories which prevail in modern science (Darwinism, for instance,) are not such as to present a reconciling view of human destiny, as after all it is but a poor outcome of the effort and labor required in penetrating the disguises of things to disover behind the scene nothing but the meaningless play of atoms ; it has come to pass that the idealism of science has been divested of much of that efficacy which at one time was ascribed to it ; and it is perceived by many, by the very ones who have tried to live on intellectualism, that it does not satisfy.

Then another substitute has been what in German is

called *Pflichtgefühl.* This word does not merely mean
doing one's duty; it describes a peculiar species of the
sentiment of duty, a kind of military promptness in an-
swering the calls of obligation, especially when imposed
by superior authority. The feeling, it seems to me,
has a background of paternalism. It rests on reverence
and respect for the constituted rulers of the land.
It has been generated, I take it, especially in the military class and the bureaucracy and from them has
spread among the people. It depends for its maintenance on confidence in the authorities, and this confidence in Germany has been considerably shaken. In
place of satisfaction and the quiet spirit of obedience
there is deep-seated, far-reaching political and social discontent. And now what I wish to say is that it is this
political and social discontent, taken in connection with
the failure of physical science or of mere intellectualism
to satisfy, that has prepared the soil for the Ethical
Movement in Germany.

There are some restless, impatient spirits, who seek to
provide a remedy for the political and social evils of
Germany by sudden and comprehensive social changes;
and it is to tne presence of this class of persons that
the spread of Socialism and its poltical strength is
due. But there are also others who realize that sudden
changes cannot be permanent and who look to a re-
newal of moral energy in the different classes of society
as the indispensable condition of achieving lasting and
beneficient results, and it was this class of persons who
have been most interested in the Ethical Movement
and most earnest in propagating it. Thus much as to
the preparation for the movement in Germany. And let

me merely add that it is a significant fact, in view of
what has just been said concerning the failure of mere
intellectualism ultimately to satisfy, that the leader of
our movement in Germany is a man of science, a man
who occupies a high position in his own department of
science, but who profoundly recognizes the need of
ethical clarification and inspiration. I allude of course
to our honored friend Prof. Foerster. The support of
such a man has been of incalculable benefit to the German Movement.

And now to speak of the results of the Congress,
there are three to which I wish to call attention. First,
the creation of an International Secretaryship which is
intended to be a means of binding together the European
societies among themselves and the European and American societies respectively. Dr. Wilhelm Foerster has
been created the first International Secretary. He is
the son of Prof. Foerster to whom I have just referred,
and the editor of the German weekly paper, *Ethische
Kultur*. He was recently arrested and condemned on
the charge of *lèse-majesté* for an article which appeared
in his paper, and was confined for several months in a
fortress. He was liberated on the eve of the assembling
of the Congress at Zurich, and was enabled to be present
at our opening meeting. He intends, as I understand,
to give his whole life to the propaganda of the Ethical
Movement.

The very considerable proportion of university professors connected with the societies is one of the characteristic features of the foreign movement. It is un-
doubtedly a source of strength, but also a source of
weakness ; because the societies must depend upon such

time as the professors can spare from their duties, and
because the university teacher, despite his most perfect
intentions, is not able to come into such immediate
contact with the feelings of the people, with the popular
interests and sentiments, as is desirable in the leaders
of Ethical Societies.

To speak, therefore, of the second result of the Congress, it is this : that it has been determined to endeavor
hereafter to follow the American plan (which the German Society at first resisted, fearing that a new ethical
clergy, as they said, might spring up) and to secure the
services of persons who will give their whole life to the
movement.   In other words, the second result has been
the decision to establish on neutral ground, in Switzerland, a college for the training of ethical leaders and
lecturers, the modest beginning of which is to be made
next summer.

Next, as to the work that has been heretofore done
by the foreign societies ; and this will give me an opportunity to speak of the third, and, to my mind, the most
valuable and important result of the Congress.   The
work done by the foreign societies thus far has consisted,
in the first place, in the holding of meetings for the discussion and explanation of the principles of the movement, especially the essential principle of all, viz., that
morality is self-centered, self-sustained, founded on
human nature, and independent of dogma, creeds, or
philosophic theories.   This idea is constantly being considered in all its bearings and the movement is being
propagated in this fashion. But, in addition, earnest
attempts have been made to testify to the ethical faith
by practical philanthropy. The German Society has .

identified itself especially with an effort to influence public opinion through the press. Whenever there is a case of injustice; whenever, through the prejudices of the ruling classes, the weak seem to be oppressed, seem to be at a disadvantage, especially in the courts, it is one of the aims of the Ethical Society to call attention to the fact and, if possible, to secure a remedy.

Particular interest has been taken by the societies in the establishment of free reading rooms. Perhaps we in this country do not quite realize how important it was to take such steps in a country like Germany, where adequate provision in this direction did not exist. The Ethical Society has rendered considerable service in the establishment of such public reading rooms, and their efforts have been recognized and sustained by the municipal authorities of Berlin.

In Austria courses of lectures have been delivered to parents on the proper training of children. And a very important investigation has been conducted into the conditions of female labor in the city of Vienna Reports of this investigation have found their way into the newspapers and have attracted great attention, and the results of the investigation will be published in detail this fall.

The Swiss Society is only a few months old and has not yet determined its plans, although there is promise of great activity.

The Italian Society is extremely interesting in many ways. I hold in my hands a pamphlet entitled " A Page from the History of Sociology; an Account of the Society for Ethical and Social Culture of Venice." This is the most important of the Italian Ethical Societies.

The object of the Society is to unite all who believe that the present industrial system is capable of modification in the direction of more perfect harmony between the social classes.   It seeks to unite persons of different beliefs and different opinions, just as we do, and men whose views are distinctly and widely divergent have in fact given their sanction to this movement.   Here, too, discussion and public meetings are one of the important instrumentalities in use.   The Venetian Society was no sooner formed than it addressed itself to the task of philanthropy, and the first scheme proposed and attempted was that of founding an asylum or shelter, a place for the amusement and instruction of the children of the working people during the hours when their parents are away in the workshops and factories.   This attempt to benefit the children was, however, vehemently denounced by the clergy of Venice.   In consequence a number of ladies who belonged to the committee in charge resigned and the enterprise had to be abandoned.

The Society then determined to address itself to the adult working people.   A college for the social and ethical culture of working people was established, the members of the Ethical Society of Venice themselves being the teachers.   This attempt met with astonishing success.   The school was opened with seven adult pupils ; after two weeks there were two hundred enrolled, and after four weeks there were four hundred, and further admittance had to be refused owing to lack of accommodation.   These classes are continued from December to May, and in the summer excursions are arranged, in which hundreds of working people take part, for the purpose of studying the art and historic monuments in which Venice is so rich, also the economic conditions, and the public institutions, especially the public charitable institutions.

Now all this is very laudable and very interesting, but it did seem to me as if there was one thing lacking in the foreign Ethical Societies—or at least if not lacking yet not sufficiently pronounced : that is, the spiritual element. I do not mean anything mystical when I use the word spiritual. When we think of morality, if we concentrate our attention on the act, on the external part of it, then we are not spiritual ; but if we care chiefly for the spirit in which the act is done, then we take the spiritual view. It seemed to me as if the spiritual side, though not wanting by any means among the leaders— in fact it was beautifully emphasized by some of the leaders—was nevertheless too much neglected ; as if the drift were in an external direction, as if the feeling prevailed that the ethical society exists for the benefit of others. I have always felt that this is a wrong attitude to take. I have always felt that an ethical society should take the ground that it exists primarily for the moral benefit of its own members. It is in this way that I have distinguished in my mind between the real members and the quasi members of an ethical society. The real member of an ethical society is the person who feels that he has not yet—morally—finished his education ; that he is in need of moral development, in need of help, and looks upon the society as a means of helping him in his moral development. The quasi member is the person who merely appreciates the society in so far as it is doing good for others. He is no real member ; at best only an ally, an associate.   Now I felt that this sort of external feeling prevails to a considerable degree in the foreign societies as it still largely exists in our own.

I went to Zurich to stand for this view, and in the opening address to the Congress, I laid the main stress upon this idea : that permanence and solidity and depth will be lacking in the Ethical Movement, and that it will not deserve to succeed unless it creates in its midst a new spirit—unless a spirit of humility be cultivated among its own members.   And the view here indicated met with the readiest response and has been expressed and embodied in the Program which the delegates adopted, as its very first paragraph, and has been made the corner-stone of the Ethical Movement, so far as the delegates who went to Zurich had the power to make it.   I will read from that Program :

The Delegates of the first International Assembly of the Federated Societies recommend to the Federated Societies of the various countries represented, the following statement, subject to future expansion and revision :

The prime aim of the Ethical Societies is to be of advantage to their own members.   The better moral life is not a gift which we are merely to confer upon others ; it is rather a difficult prize which we are to try with unwearying and unceasing effort to secure for ourselves.   The means which are to serve to this end are : first, the close contact into which our associations bring us with others having the same purpose in view ; second, the moral education and instruction of the young in the ethical principles, which in their foundations are independent of all dogmatic presupposition ; third, guidance for adults in the task of moral self-education.

Furthermore, the Ethical Societies should define their attitude toward the great social questions of the present day, in the solution of which the part to be played by the moral forces of society is of the highest significance.

We recognize that the efforts of the masses of the people to obtain a more humane existence, imply a moral aim of the greatest importance, and we consider it our duty to second these efforts with all possible earnestness and to the full extent of our ability. We believe, however, that the evil to be remedied is not only the material need of the poor, but that an evil hardly less serious is to be found in the moral need which exists among the wealthy, who are often deeply imperiled in their moral integrity by the discords in which the defects of the present industrial system involve them.

We regard resistance to wrong and oppression as a sacred duty, and believe that under existing circumstances conflict is still indispensable as a means of clarifying men's ideas of right and of obtaining better conditions. We demand, however, that the conflict be carried on within the limits prescribed by morality, in the interest of society as a whole and with a constant eye to the final establishment of social peace as the supreme consummation.

We expect of the organs of the Ethical Federation that they will endeavor to provide, so far as they are able, intellectual armor to serve in the social struggle—by this we mean the publication of careful scientific treatises, which shall have for their object to ascertain whether the positions of individualism and socialism are not susceptible of being united in a deeper philosophy of life ; further, statistical investigations to show with the impressiveness of facts how profoundly our present conditions are in need of reform, and furthermore to see to it that the results thus obtained shall be spread far and wide so that the public conscience may be developed in the direction of a higher social justice.

We leave it to the several societies, according to the particular circumstances of the countries to which they belong, to carry out the above general purpose in particular ways ; but we especially call upon all the members of the various societies, in their individual capacity, to promote the progressive social movement of the times by simplicity in the conduct of life and by the display of an active public spirit.

We recognize the institution of pure monogamic marriage as a priceless possession of mankind, indispensable for the moral development of the individual and for the permanent existence of civilization ; but we demand that the monogamic idea shall express itself in the sentiments and practice of men with a degree of consistency which to a very great extent is still wanting.

We demand for woman opportunity for the fullest development of her mental and moral personality, and realizing that her personality is of equal worth with that of man, we pledge ourselves, as far as we are able, to secure the recognition of this equality in every department of life.

We regard especially the lot of female wage earners in industrial establishments and in personal service as one of the most grievous evils of the present time, and we will use such influence as we possess to restore to all classes of the population the conditions upon which a true home life depends.

We regard it as a fundamental task of modern civilization to give back to the educational system the unity which it has in a a large measure lost, and to replace the missing key-stone once supplied by dogmatic teaching in schools and universities by setting up a common ethical purpose as the aim of all culture.

We heartily appreciate the efforts now being made to bring about universal peace among the nations, and we would contribute our share towards the success of these efforts by inwardly overcoming the military spirit, by endeavoring to counteract the attraction that military glory exerts on the minds of the young, and by seeking to provide that the ethically valuable elements which the military system contains may find expression in nobler and worthier forms.

Furthermore, we would oppose that national egotism and national passion, which at the present day are just as dangerous foes of peace as are the prejudices and interests of the governing classes ; and in times of excitement and of political hatred we will exert ourselves in conjunction with others who think as we do, to compel attention to the voice of reason and of conscience.

We ask our Ethical Societies not only to direct their attention toward the outward extension of the movement, but to devote their utmost energy to the building up of a new ideal of life, which shall correspond to the demands of enlightened thinking, feeling and living, confident that such an ideal for which mankind is thirsting will in the end be of equal profit to all classes and to all nations.

We are not a Pythagorean society; we are not a band of stoics; we are not a company of recluses who stand aloof from the concerns of life. We recognize that we are to grapple with the social and political questions of the day, because only by endeavoring to lift these heavy weights will our own moral fiber become strong and firm. But, nevertheless, our moral growth is still the principal aim. We can grow morally only in so far as we take an interest in the moral concerns of the community. But, on the other hand, it is equally true and equally to be emphasized that, so far as we are concerned, we shall endeavor to solve the great social questions, the great public questions, by changes which we effect in ourselves. We are to regenerate society primarily by regenerating the one individual member of society for whom we are responsible.

This is the difference between an ethical society and the peace societies, the social reform societies, the educational societies and the others—that they chiefly lay stress upon what the government ought to do or upon what other people ought to do, or in general upon how the world is to be set aright, while the ethical society, mindful also of these demands, yet lays its chief stress upon the question, What am I to do? How shall I set the world right by setting myself right? And this note dominates the entire Statement of Principles which I have read.

For instance, it is said that the Ethical Society must

take an interest in the labor question, and immediately
we are asked to co-operate in the social movement of
the time by leading simple lives.   The material distress
of the poor is a great evil, but the unease of conscience,
in view of the fact that we enjoy exceptional, undeserved
advantages, is also a great evil which we must try to
remedy.   And we must try to remedy it, not by blunt-
ing our moral susceptibilities, but by making them still
more keen.

Again the platform insists upon the institution of
monogamic marriage as a priceless possession, and it
goes on to tell us that the idea of monogamy is not expressed in the sentiment and practice of mankind as it
should be ; whereby is meant that men ought to be faithful to the ideal of women before marriage as well as in
marriage, just as women, conversely, are expected to be
faithful on their side.

Even where mention is made of so public a concern
as international peace we are yet urged to contribute to
it as individuals by trying to counteract the attraction
of military glory, by overcoming that hatred of foreigners
to which we are all liable, and by stopping at this source
those passions which lead to national frenzy and international war.

I have come back with fresh inspiration and fresh
confidence, with an exhilarating sense of a wider broth-
erhood, with the feeling that though oceans roll between us, and the barriers of speech and traditions and
sentiment may seem to separate us, yet in the essential
purpose our friends abroad and we are one.   I wish I
could communicate this feeling of a wider union to you.
It would possibly have gratified your pride could you

have listened to the ample and generous acknowledg-
ments which the delegates made of what they conceived
to be their indebtedness to the American Ethical Societies. But I confess that a feeling very unlike that
of flattered pride was uppermost in my mind as I
listened to those words of recognition. It was rather a
grave and heavy sense of responsibility, because our
foreign friends are very glad to hear of such success as
you have met with. They are also willing to learn from
your example, so far as it is a worthy one,; but they are
disposed to scrutinize you with a searching carefulness
such as possibly you have no conception of; because
this is what they say to themselves : " We look to the
ethical idea with hope ; we look to it as something that
is to be a means of salvation in the midst of the political and social whirlwinds that are likely to sweep over
society ; we look to it with hope, but we want to see
whether it is worthy of our confidence. And, how are
we to determine ? Why, we will scrutinize the lives of
the members of these Ethical Societies in America. The
Ethical Movement has existed in America for twenty
years. In twenty years the ethical idea must have taken
root and borne fruit. What are the fruits which it has
borne ? "

What are the ethical fruits—not how large are the
revenues or the audiences ? but what are the fruits that
appear in the life of the Society? Are the merchants
of the Ethical Society, as a rule, stricter in their views
than their competitors, or are they like others—good,
bad and indifferent? Are the relations between masters
and men characterized by a keener sense of right and
a more careful considerateness, and, when there are

faults on one side or the other, by a greater charity ?
Are our children educated on nobler principles and in
finer ways ?

Oh, my friends, let us at least try to be able to meet
these questions.

www.ingramcontent.com/pod-product-compliance
Lightning Source LLC
Chambersburg PA
CBHW030011030726
47499CB00008B/2997